Jackie Morris lives in a small house by the sea in Pembrokeshire, Wales, where she writes and paints. She has two children, Tom and Hannah, a small pack of dogs and a small pride of cats. Her internationally bestselling picture books for Frances Lincoln include *I am Cat, Tell me a Dragon, Lord of the Forest, The Snow Leopard, The Seal Children, Can You See a Little Bear?, The Cat and the Fiddle – A Treasury of Nursery Rhymes*, and *How the Whale Became* by Ted Hughes. She has also written and illustrated a critically acclaimed novel for older children, *East of the Sun, West of the Moon*.

You can find out more about Jackie Morris and her books at www.jackiemorris.co.uk

For Sophie, Jon, Rhoderic, Thomas and Katie.
For all of you, with love from me.

JANETTA OTTER-BARRY BOOKS

Text and illustrations copyright © Jackie Morris 2010

First published in Great Britain and in the USA in 2010 by
Frances Lincoln Children's Books,
74-77 White Lion Street, London N1 9PF
www.franceslincoln.com

First paperback published in Great Britain in 2014

A catalogue record for this book is available
from the British Library.

ISBN 978-1-84780-457-0

Illustrated with watercolours

Printed in China

9 8 7 6 5 4 3 2 1

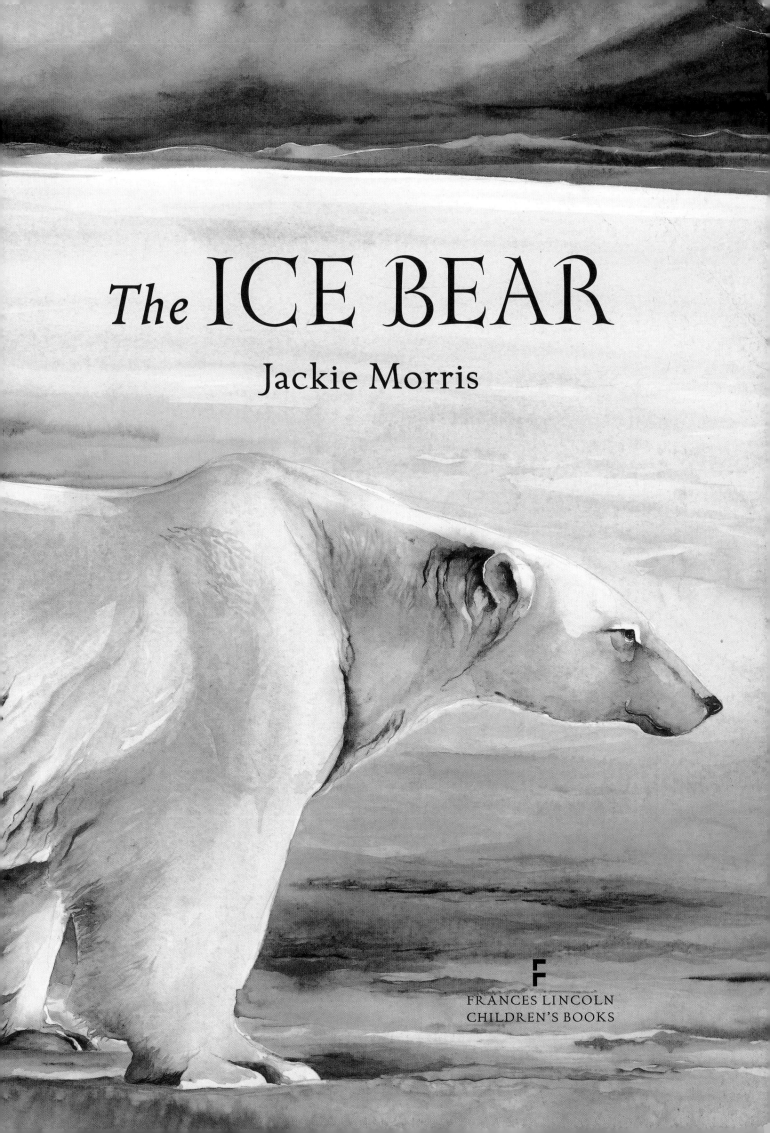

The ICE BEAR

Jackie Morris

F

FRANCES LINCOLN
CHILDREN'S BOOKS

In the beginning of time people and animals lived together on the earth and there was no difference between them. Bear, human, raven, fox, even snow and ice, all had spirit, all had soul. The air was pure and clear as crystal. Words held a magic. A word spoken in a chance, a wish or a whisper would hold a magic that would shape the world.

Into this world they were born, in the dark months, when the cold and the wind turned water to stone. So small. She held them close to keep them warm in the blue ice cave that was their world.

But Raven tricked her. She stole away one child, carried him
high into the darkness of winter, over the frozen sea.
The bear wept when she found that her cub had gone.
Her ice tears formed scars on her cheeks.
She held her one child safer and closer and waited for
the sun to rise. But she never forgot.

Far away the hunter hurried home. He could smell the storm coming, the scent of snow on the knife-edge of the wind. His last hunt before true winter. He had seals and a few hares to last until the sun rose again.

He heard the deep cry of the raven, saw the black shape in the distance. The bird flew up as he drew closer, and there on the ground was a bundle wrapped in a scrap of white fur. He scooped up the fur on to the sledge and hurried for home as the storm snapped its teeth at his heels.

The storm came in fast but his dogs moved faster.

Safe home at last they stored the food for the dark days ahead.

They honoured the spirits of the hare and the seal,

then they unwrapped the bundle of cream white fur.

Two eyes, black as midwinter.

Dark hair like a raven's wing.

Two hands, fingers clawed by the cold.

A child.

For seven years they had longed for a child.

His mother made him a parka of seal skin.

She lined it with the fur of the white wolf and decorated it

with patterns of coloured beads and the white tails of ermine.

For seven years they held him close, sang him songs and lullabies.

They sang to him of the seal and the whale, the owl and the fox.

They sang of the snow and the ice and the wind, of summer and winter,

of darkness and light. He loved the stories and he loved

the songs, the language of ice and the song of the wind.

Most of all he loved to hear of the great white bears.

And they loved him.

He seldom spoke. He often smiled.

And always the raven watched over him.

It was the end of the summer of his seventh year.
His father was hunting with his bone-tipped spear.
His mother was taking in the last of the harvest
of seal meat and whale.

He saw in the snow a pale shard of shining light.
A piece of amber, smoothed by the oceans, coloured,
clear and beautiful, like a fragment of fire, washed ashore
from a far-off place. A seal's length away, another, and as he looked
he saw a trail of shining amber, bright jewels on the hard-packed snow.
He thought they were fallen stars.

He followed the trail, picking up each shining piece, cupping them
in his mittens. His mother would love them.
As he stooped to pick up the brightest and best,
in flew the raven and snatched it away.

Raven flew over the ice, the length of four canoes.
She dropped the treasure and it lay like a flame on the cold white.
The boy moved to take it, and in flew the bird. It became a dance,
boy and raven. As if enchanted by the raven's game the boy
followed the bird, out on to the snow and away from home.

It was a while before he looked around and realised that
he did not know the way back. The wind had blown
a fresh dusting of snow over his footprints.

He was lost.

The boy looked around. The sun was low in the sky.
He walked towards the sun, towards where he thought home was,
still clutching the smooth beads of amber. He walked over ice ridges
and down into valleys. The cold clung to him, it gnawed at him
and fear began to suck at his bones.

He walked, but nothing now seemed familiar to him.
The sun set, then rose and set again. It took moments.
Winter had come. Stars began to fill the sky.

He sank into thin powder snow, climbed out and walked on,
until his small strength was gone.

He fell to his knees, head bowed against the bright whiteness
of the snow, and a weary sleep began to overwhelm his heart.

It was then that they came for him.

He heard them first, the soft paw pad on powder snow,
a hiss of hot breath in the dry, cold air, the flick of an ear.
He lifted his head and shaded his eyes with a mittened hand.
All around him it seemed the snow had come to life.
He knew now that he must die.

As he reached out a hand to the biggest of the bears
the amber treasure fell to the snow.
And as the bear breathed in the child's scent
he heard in his heart the word "brother".

For a moment boy and bear remembered, far back,
an echo of a memory, the great white bear who had
held them close in the blue ice cave.
Then the boy thought of his mother
and father, even as Brother Bear rubbed his
great head against the child, then lifted him on to
his back.

Fast as the wind the boy and seven bears
set off across the frozen sea.

His father followed.

He traced the shadow of the tracks of the boy,
a shift in the snow here, a mark of a hand there, hardly a trail.

He came to the place where the boy had sunk to his knees.
All around in a circle of chaos the sign of the bears filled him
with sorrow. He saw where the amber had fallen, and his heart
cracked like summer ice. He stood, alone in the white land
and made a promise to the memory of the child.

He would kill the bear that had taken the life of his child.

The boy clung tight to the silver white bear as they ran
like the wind over the frozen sea, golden in starlight.
Above, the stars of the Caribou shone down.

They came to a place, a hill of ice. As he slid to the ground
the hill raised its head. A giant of a bear, yellow white fur,
black eyes. Ridges of scars from tears of ice marked her face.
The boy reached out a hand to touch, and traced down the scar
as the great bear breathed in his scent.

This was her son, her stolen child.

She held him close, the lost one. He buried his face in her golden white fur,
breathed in deep the rich smell of his mother, and the memory of the ice cave,
so long ago, flooded back into his mind.

All the while the hunter drew closer. Maddened by grief he followed the trail
of the running bears, a river of paw prints on the frozen sea.
Ice tears burnt on his face, blurring his vision.
He came to the gathering and ran into the ring of bears,
raising his bone-tipped spear to strike a killing blow.

High above, Raven called.

The boy looked up to see his father, and the spear.
He flung himself between the man and the bear.
Raven's cry broke the spell of bloodlust
and the hunter's spear tumbled as he scooped up the child.

Around the three, the white bears circled, heads swaying,
waiting for a sign from the great she bear. But she rose,
knelt before the hunter and the child.
She thanked him for the care he had
shown to her cub. Now he was home,
she said, and would stay with
his people, the bear people.

In turn the hunter knelt and thanked the she bear for keeping his child safe. Now he had found him he would take him home to his people.

The boy stood between the man and the bear.

He felt that his heart was torn.
He wanted to stay with the bears.
He wanted to go with his father.

The child ran his mittened hand over the bead patterns
of his parka. "I will stay with the bears in the winter,
when the sky is dark and life is hard."
His father held back a sob in his throat, eyes hot with tears.
"And I will live with the people in the summer," the boy said.
"We will hunt together."

The great bear took her son's head in her fur-fringed paws and breathed into him three times. He felt himself changing, muscle and bone, tooth and claw. Together they carried the hunter back to his home by the fast freezing sea.

From that day the child lived as a bear through the winter and as he grew he learned the ways of the bears. In summer he lived with the people and taught them the wisdom of bears. In the dark times of winter his human mother would hang his moccasins close by the fire. She would sing to her children of the first one, the magical shapeshifter, child of her wishes.

Out on the ice the great white bear would raise his head to the stars and watch the dance of the Northern Lights.

One spirit, one heart, one soul, one people.

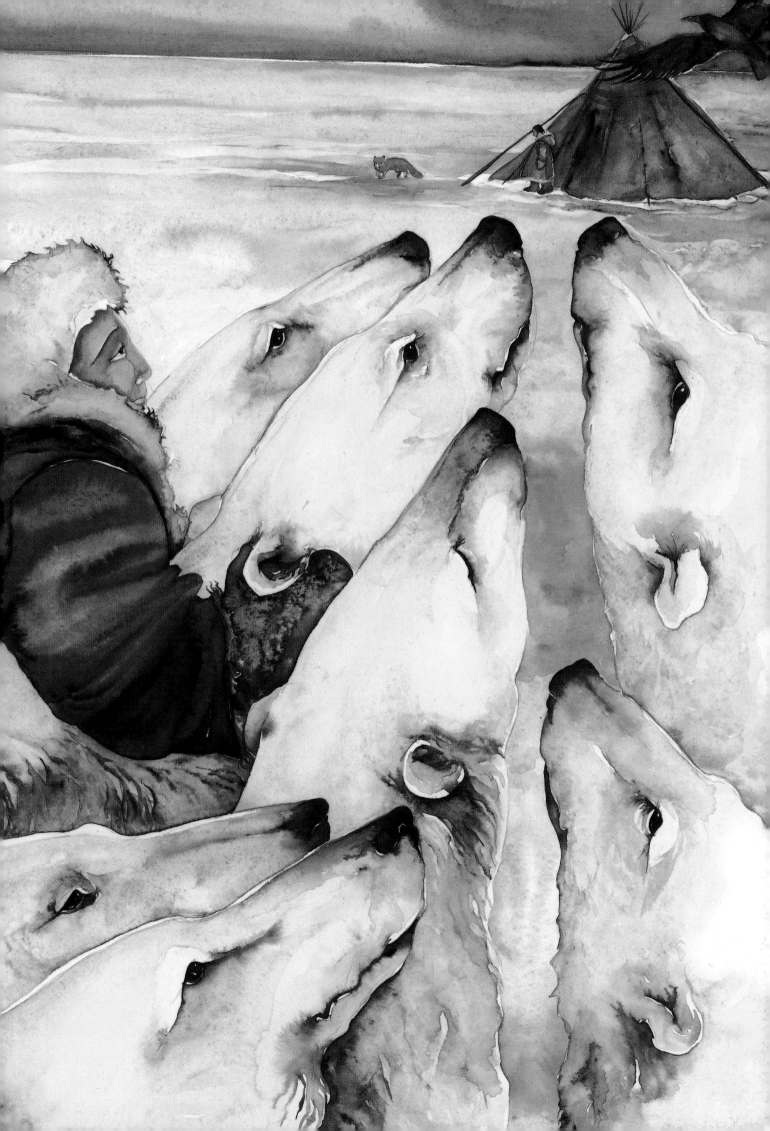

MORE BEAUTIFUL PICTURE BOOKS BY JACKIE MORRIS
FROM FRANCES LINCOLN CHILDREN'S BOOKS

I AM CAT

"The superb illustrations show every intricate detail of each cat in its own habitat, so that you feel you are on safari watching the real thing, utterly mesmerised…" *School Librarian*

THE SNOW LEOPARD

"Ravishing paintings" – *Sunday Telegraph*
"A gorgeous fantasy" – *The New York Times*

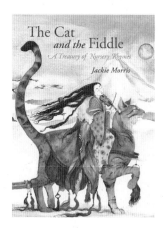

THE CAT AND THE FIDDLE
A Treasury of Nursery Rhymes

"This sumptuous collection is one to pore over, cherish and return to again and again. A lovely book." *Marilyn Brocklehurst, Bookseller*

TELL ME A DRAGON

"The ultimate dragon book portrays every kind of dragon a child can imagine. A magical story which children will delight in." *Bookseller*

Frances Lincoln titles are available from all good bookshops.
You can also buy books and find out more about your favourite titles,
authors and illustrators on our website: www.franceslincoln.com